To My lovely Granddaughter
Taybree

I hope you will always love
being a Mother. It is the
best!   With love,
            Grandma Miller

I Want to Be a
MOMMY

....————ℓℓℓℓℓ————...

To my grandmas, my mom, my daughters,
and my granddaughters, and to all who
want to grow up to be a mommy

Visit us at ShadowMountain.com

Library of Congress Cataloging-in-Publication Data

Cooley, Judy, author, illustrator.
  I want to be a mommy / written and illustrated by Judy Cooley.
      pages cm
  Summary: A little girl thinks of all the things she could be and do as she grows up and decides that being a mommy includes all of those things.
  ISBN 978-1-60908-910-8 (hardbound : alk. paper)
  [1. Occupations—Fiction. 2. Mother and child—Fiction.] I. Title.
  PZ7.C7766Iaj 2012
  [E]—dc23   2011044044

Printed in Canada   03/2012
Friesens, Manitoba, Canada

10   9   8   7   6   5   4   3   2   1

I Want to Be a MOMMY

Written and Illustrated by
Judy Cooley

SHADOW
MOUNTAIN

My mommy says I can be anything I want to be when I grow up.

So, I want to be a princess. I'll wear beautiful dresses and live in a castle . . . but then I can't play in the dirt.

Hmm, I want to be more than a princess.

I want to be an explorer when I grow up. I'll stomp in the mud and climb big mountains . . . but what if I get hurt?

Hmm, I want to be more than an explorer.

I want to be a doctor when I grow up. I'll take care of babies and kiss their owies better . . . but then I'll need to learn big words like "stethoscope."

Hmm, I want to
be more than a
doctor.

TREASURE ISLAND

All The Adventure of Dick and Jane and Friends

I want to be a teacher when I grow up. I'll use big words and know the answers to almost everything . . . but then I won't get recess.

Hmm, I want to be more than a teacher.

I want to be a clown when I grow up. I'll teach tricks to the animals and juggle . . . but I'm scared of riding on an elephant.

Hmm, I want to be more than a clown.

I want to be a cowgirl when I grow up. I'll be brave as I ride on my horse and rope the stars . . . but my rope can't reach the stars.

Hmm, I want to be more than a cowgirl.

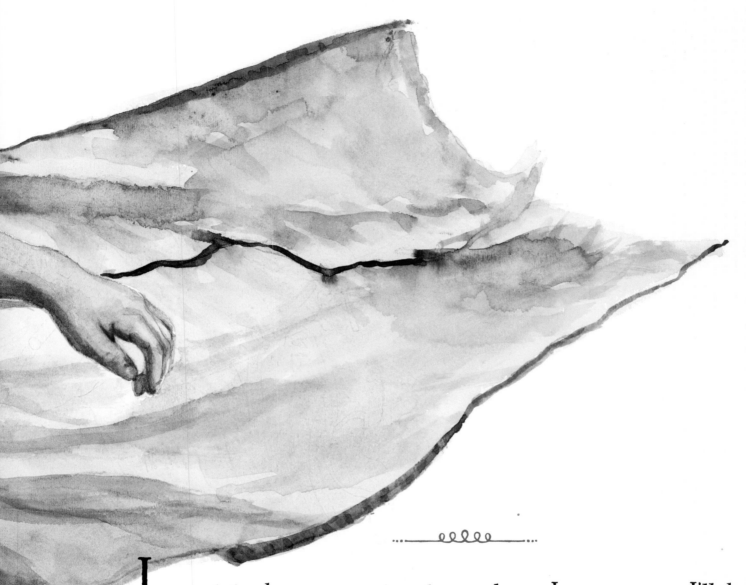

I want to be a movie star when I grow up. I'll be the hero in the movie and save the day . . . but then I might have to do all that mushy, kissy stuff.

Hmm, I want to be more than a movie star.

I want to be a famous
singer when I grow up!
I'll sing so nicely and
then blow kisses and
take a bow . . . but what
if I lose my voice?

Hmm, I want to be more than a famous singer.

I want to be a mermaid when I grow up. I'll sing with the whales and swim in the ocean . . . but then I can't run and dance.

Hmm, I want to be more than a mermaid.

I want to be the world's fastest runner when I grow up. I'll win the gold medal and meet the president . . . but what if I get too tired?

Hmm, I want to be more than the fastest runner.

I want to be the president when I grow up. I'll tell everyone to be nice and say the Pledge of Allegiance . . . but what happens when I can't make everyone happy?

Hmm, I want to be more than the president.

I want to be a magic fairy when I grow up. I'll fly around and make wishes come true.

But Mommy says I can be ANYTHING I want to be. So . . .

I want to be a mommy when I grow up because mommies can do everything!

They can climb mountains, kiss owies, know everything, juggle, ride horses, save the day, sing beautifully, swim and run really fast, tell everyone to be nice, and make wishes come true. And a mommy is a princess who can play in the dirt too. So, I want to be a mommy when I grow up!

I asked Mommy what she wants to be when I grow up. And she said

A GRANDMA! ♡